This book is all about . . .

Photo of me

Baby Grows Up

with

Peter Rabbit

A record of baby's first year

Frederick Warne

Waiting for baby

How we felt in the weeks before your arrival

What we did to get ready

Ideas for names

First saw baby on the ultrasound scan

First heard baby's heartbeat

First felt baby move

Baby's pre-natal scan

Baby's birth

My name is ....

I was born on ....

Time ....

Place ....

I weighed ....

My eyes were ....

My hair was ....

Photo

My first photo

Baby's first days

I came home on

Photo

This is a photo of me when I arrived home

Use this page to write about baby's
first days at home

Baby's first visitors

My first visitors

Some of the gifts given to me

Photo of my visitors

Baby loves peek-a-boo games

Favorite things

My favorite toys

Photo of me with my toys

Baby loves bright colors

peter loves radishes

My favorite nursery rhyme

My favorite song

My favorite game

Bathtime

My first time in the bath

My favorite bath toys

My favorite bath song

Photo of me in the bath

A bathtime song for baby . . .

Splish splash, splish splash,
Rub-a-dub dub
Splash, splish, splash, splish,
Baby's in the tub!

Bedtime

My bedtime routine

I first slept through the night on

Photo of me in my crib

My favorite bedtime story

My favorite crib toys

Eating

I was first weaned from the breast / bottle when I was
_____ months and _____ weeks

The first pureed food I ever tasted _____

I was eating finger food when I was
_____ months and _____ weeks

My favorite food _____

My least favorite food _____

Photo of me in my high chair

I first held a spoon _____

I fed myself _____

I drank from a cup _____

Hands and feet

Here is my first handprint
I was _____ weeks old

A tickling game for baby . . .

Walk your fingers slowly up baby's front.

slowly, slowly, very slowly, Creeps the garden snail. slowly, slowly, very slowly, Up the wooden rail.

ery quickly

little mouse.

ly, quickly, very quickly

Round about the house.

Tickle baby throughout this verse.

Here is my first footprint
I was   weeks old

On the move

I lifted my head

I reached for things

I rolled over

I sat up

I crawled on my knees

I pulled myself up

My first steps

Photo of me crawling

Special occasions

Decorate these pages with photos and write about special occasions in baby's first year

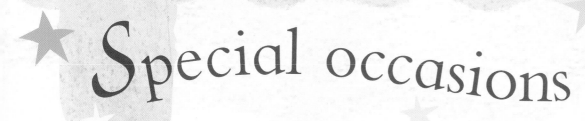

Special occasions

Days out

My first day out was to _____

I was _____ months and _____ weeks old

I went with _____

What we did there _____

_____

My favorite activities _____

_____

Special things that happened _____

_____

_____

Photo

This is a photo of me on my day out

Talking

I smiled

I laughed

I babbled

I copied noises

Tweet Tweet
Tweet

Eeek!

I started understanding words

My first words

Some funny things I said

Baby's health

I have been immunized against . . .
Immunization   Date

Childhood illnesses

Allergies

This is when my first teeth came through . . .

1 _____

2 _____

3 _____

4 _____

5 _____

6 _____

7 _____

8 _____

9 _____

10 _____

Upper

Right

Left

Lower

11 _____

12 _____

13 _____

14 _____

15 _____

16 _____

17 _____

18 _____

19 _____

20 _____

When the first tooth appears, write in the date next to the number 1 on the list below. Then number the relevant tooth on the diagram, and so on.

Height and weight chart

Month	Weight	Height
1		
2		
3		
4		
5		
6		
7		
8		
9		
10		
11		
12		

A baby bouncing game . . .

See the little Robin

Sitting in the tree.

Bounce baby astride your knee

Flutter flutter go his wings,

Take a look at me!

Wave baby's arms up and down.

My family tree

Grandfather Grandmother   Grandfather Grandmother

Aunts   Uncles   Aunts   Uncles

Father   Mother

Brothers   Sisters

Me

Photo of my family

Baby's first birthday

How we celebrated

Who joined in

My presents

Use the space on this page to write about the day

Photo of me on my birthday

Photos

Photos

FREDERICK WARNE

Published by the Penguin Group
Penguin Books Ltd, 27 Wrights Lane, London W8 5TZ, England
Penguin Putnam Inc., 375 Hudson Street, New York, N.Y. 10014, USA
Penguin Books Canada Ltd, 10 Alcorn Avenue, Toronto, Ontario, Canada M4V 3B2
Penguin Books (NZ) Ltd, Private Bag 102902, NSMC, Auckland, New Zealand
Penguin Books India (P) Ltd, 11 Community Centre, Panchsheel Park, New Delhi 110 017, India
Penguin Books (South Africa) (Pty) Ltd, 5 Watkins Street, Denver Ext 4, Johannesburg 2094, South Africa

Penguin Books Ltd, Registered Offices: Harmondsworth, Middlesex, England

Visit our web site at: www.peterrabbit.com

First published by Frederick Warne 2001
3 5 7 9 10 8 6 4 2

Copyright © Frederick Warne & Co., 2001

ISBN 0 7232 4802 8

Artwork by Alex Vining

Colour reproduction by Saxon Photolitho
Printed and bound in Singapore by Tien Wah Press (Pte) Ltd